The Legend of Quicksilver

Enlightenment Book I

By:

Michael P. Faraday

Quicksilver

QuickSilver

The Silver Dragon Inc.

&

Michael P. Faraday

Ashcroft St. Auburn, MA 01501

ISBN:

**ISBN-13:978-0692395745
(Michael P. Faraday)**

Printed & published in the United
States of America, in North Charleston
South Carolina.

Chapter's

Quote

"To be considered a great man you must be able to bring joy to others, for then you will be remembered as a legend."

By:

Quicksilver: Michael P. Faraday

Author's forward

The year is 2012, During a period of time when society is turned upside down a lone figure appears from the wake of fire's brimstone, and through ideals of ancient rituals turns despair into hope.

Unknown to this modern World an everlasting war has been plaguing the universe.

It is the trials and tribulations of time endured that in the end …

Martial Science reigns supreme!

Chapter one

Shadows of 2012

The 1st decade of the new millennium had past. Now coming into the year of 2012 it was for told the end of our World was imminent!

The negligence and greed of man had the society, for which we live in, turned upside down.

Moral character was only considered in passing as a relic of a civilized World that had been forgotten.

Lied to by our government of gathered Nations, and then being sheltered into a life of material objects in the order of a status quo the real truth was oblique.

The petty violence of all the religious movements in that of war was nothing compared to the bigger picture of what awaited us all!

There is a reason, without any doubt Heaven and Hell did exist.

However; by its own concept into reality of man himself the vision to see this was masked.

For now it was greed and corruption to start. The next step was Natural Disaster and sickness of untold disease.

It was at this point my story shall now begin ...

Chapter two

Central America

Deep within in the jungles of Costa Rica a folklore tale of a nomad of mysterious powers was believed by many to roam from village to village.

Legend says his face was never shown, and his voice was never heard.

It was also said he came into sight only after hostile Gorilla Rebels had wiped-out most of the life in the village they plundered.

The smoke and putrid odors of rotting flesh... all the cries of hope waited for vengeance to come!

For those who were left behind after the aftermath were now faced to rebuild once more.

Then he came. They called him Van, because he appeared out of nowhere, and as quickly he came.

Then he vanished; without a trace. Into the darkness from which he came.

The stories of Van are like in many other myths there are many interpretations of him.

Such as the nomad, a lost soul, the warrior, the protector, perhaps even a God?

One thing was for certain and that was that he was in fact mysterious.

Also he seemed to always be in search for something in particular.

What that might be was not apparently clear. Well at least for the time being anyways.

Chapter three

Zenzar Bar

One of the last remaining free villages by the sea lays Zenzar Bar.

This island is Pristine in natural beauty & was somewhat secluded from the rest of the World.

The sea was on one side and treacherous mountains on the other.

Created by one of the Great Earthquakes this village was known to only a few.

The only way you could reach this place of wonder was threw the Great Water Falls of Tori.

Where a secret passage lay behind the cascading of cold, nail driven flow of pouring water from above!

Once you made it past this point, in the distance you saw a small glowing pool.

Chapter four

Visitors From Above

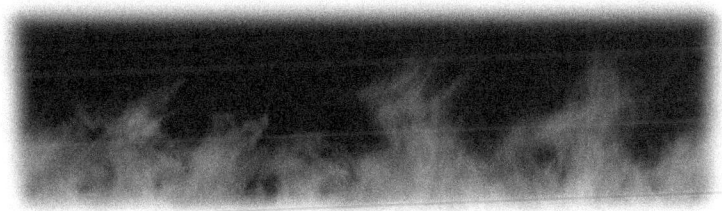

On what began as a usual morning in the fifth month, on the 12th day soon became what was referred to as the End of Days!

As the villagers started their morning routines they were preparing breakfast and setting-up all the nets for the daily fishing in the lagoon. All seemed to be normal.

Suddenly the sky now turned jet black. As if night had fallen, and blocked out the sunlight!

Then the wind began to blow wildly followed by a very terrifying sound! As shadowy figures fell from the sky!

Next it seemed as if hell had consumed Earth, and the cries of death began to echo throughout this once peaceful village by the sea.

Next dark shadow silhouettes fell from the sky. Panic ran ramped throughout the small peaceful village.

Through their own fear's they trampled one another franticly to find cover.

Fire was seen blowing through the sky as it touched down on their thatched dwellings.

As the villagers then watched in horror quickly did the fires burn their homes down to the ground?

All was lost as the fire and the smoke encumbered the screams for mercy!

Then a flash of defiance light glimmered through the sight of all this death, and there he stood.

The legend of the told folklore stories himself; as he walked along the path of destruction ...

His head rose up to look upon him was never heard of before.

Although he did resembled the figure of a man it was as though his face was still unclear?

Was this figure to be our savior? Could it really be him? Then he spoke!

Chapter five

Orphans

Fate

"All society has for truth is bleached lies. A fresh start is in need! May the spirit of mind, body, and soul educate these two? "

When the daylight returned back to that of a clear sky, and warm rays of light touched the face of those who were left behind …

There slightly off to one-side sat two very special young children. One girl named Sam and one boy named Silver.

Their parents were killed by whatever the visitors from the sky above were?

Let it also be known that neither of these children was related. Both of them came from opposite sides of the village.

Next these two children were taken by this mysterious God like Van, and never seen again.

As quickly as he had appeared, and vanquished the visitors who wreaked havoc to this small subjugated village did he also vanish; with Sam and Silver!

Chapter six

The Islands of Ryu Kyu

Far to the east lay a chain of small islands. These islands are set between China and Japan.

As it happens one of these islands was non inhabitable. This was because of all its volcanic activity. This kept almost everyone away.

Not to mention the impossible Coral Reef which encompassed its shoreline too.

It is here that Sam and Silver would begin their new life; in preparation to save the fate of the World!

The first several years were spent listening to the legends of folklore and stories. Then they learned to understand some of the simple tasks of learning communication.

They were well taken care of in every means, and by the young age of five both children could speak quite well.

It was at this point they needed to start learning The Way. This is described as the union of the mind fused together with the body to enhance that of balance to harmony.

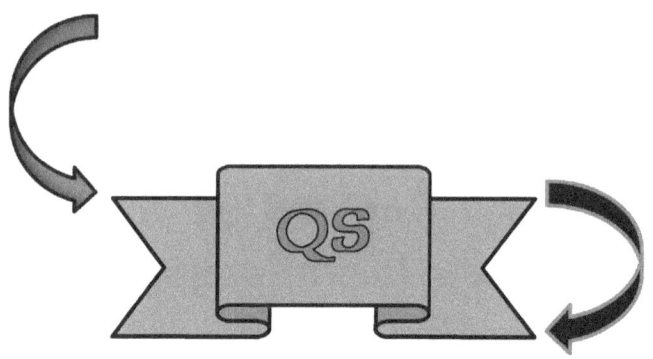

Chapter seven

Let the Training Begin

The next ten years of their training a foundation of discipline was built and instilled into Sam and Silver.

They had known nothing of the outside World or what it was evolving into.

Material possessions were of no concern to them. To live they worked the land by planting and harvesting crops of splendor in fruits and vegetables.

For meat they had an endless bounty at their very fingertips of fresh fish, and shellfish too.

Entertainment came by their means of learning different music from trials, and tribulations from their many assorted endeavors.

With Van they learned the artistry of **calligraphy;** they also painted pictures of nature from the landscape around their small island.

They exercised one third of each day also they learned the science of Physics another third of the day.

Before each start and at the end of each day they practiced the art of meditation.

Lastly with all these aspects combined they learned about the importance of **vitality**.

Then Sam and Silver learned how it related to not only structure, but in the powers of healing as well.

What these selected children were in fact learning was how to live in the Martial Way.

The Martial Way is a way of peace before war, and it is also the learning about virtue into patience in regards to knowing ... How ~ When ~ Where & Why.

Chapter eight

The Power of Meditation

Kneeling beside Van; one to each side the three of them faced the rising sun as it came up over the sea early in the mornings.

Then this practice was repeated in the evenings on top of the highest point where the volcano was.

As they placed their hands together and bowed their heads they then closed their eyes as their pulse began to slow.

A total concentration of centralization to harmony was given full attention at this point and time.

Van the master spoke first, and then his words were repeated by Sam and Silver in sequence.

Taikyokuken

Ken Sho Ryu is our Art.

If we should ever have to use our Art may our spirit guide us?

Effort is our means ...

Etiquette is our way ...

Character is our being ...

Sincerity is our passion ...

{Meditation had now begun}

Then after a long pause of silence where they cleared their minds, and focused upon values of virtue ...

~ Self-control is our domain! ~

Now their training into the Art of peaceful re-direction of war had begun.

Their first segment in practice consisted of exercise of endurance.

Starting from the beach in the mornings hot; hot sun they had to run through the jungle up to the ridge of the largest volcano on the island.

Once they reached this ridge they went into a push-up position, and held this form while gazing into the massive crater of bubbling hot glowing lava.

This was the time to hold conversation of thoughts to one another.

Once all three spoke their peace Van always ended with ...

"" The trouble that affects you is pain. Pain is good. It makes you feel alive and full of spirit! ""

"" But pain is also a sign of weakness! The more pain you feel each day is more weakness that is in fact leaving your body.

So my children work hard in everything you do, and let your pain wash away from your body and your soul. ""

Then they ran back through the jungle where they climbed vines that rose hundreds of feet above the ground below.

Next they went to what they called the Working Tree. This tree was massive in size with all different levels of branches; which formed their levels of skill to be acquired.

They also ran along channels of uneven lengths to learn their balance too. They hung upside down and did countless sit-up's, for what seemed to be hours!

They punched and kicked the wide base of this tree till the blood flowed down their fatigued limbs!

Smashing their arms and chins over and over, and over again against the course rough branches!

The second segment took place after a short meal at lunch time.

During this time period they combated against each other learning the accurate point of vitality within the body.

This portion was referred to as The Relation of Physics.

Where early in the morning they beat on the Working Tree and their own bodies.

Here they beat on each other trying finding ways to subdue one another as quickly and as efficiently as *possible*.

By using the ancient text of old forum the Liberal Arts of:

Boxing ~ Kenpo ~ Karate ~ Judo ~ *Jujitsu* ~ & Kung – Fu.

Before completing the day's events of exercises before they ate dinner; they would swim out in the fury of the sea where *its* waves pounded and crashed harshly against that of the reef.

It is here where they were now expected to find a single pearl from the bounty of the sea; *before* swimming back to the shore for their supper.

This was how they spent every day of their lives, and this cycle was never broken for any reason at all.

Chapter nine

The Flickering Flame

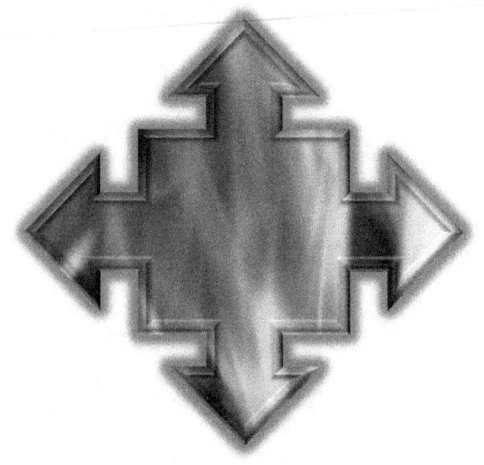

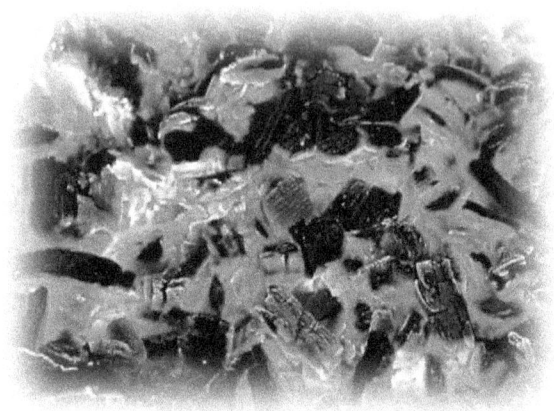

Night fell late in the evening on the island. Along with this it also brought a sense of mystery along with it.

The sounds of the jungle could be eerie to those who are not accustomed, and the mist that came in from the spray of the ocean was so heavy you had to part it to advance through.

The only visible sight was that of the flicker of the single fire which was the only light seen; every night at dusk.

It was at this time we played the game. Set on a mat in front of the flame laid a variety of what we called toys.

In toys I mean weapons of skill in the Orient culture. Such as Swords, Kamas, Nunchaku, Assorted knifes, Throwing stars, Staffs, as well as other various instruments of warfare.

Any and all weapons of which you learned to yield you must not only master their expertise, but learn how to respect their nature too.

So first we selected a choice. Then we were given a specific time to learn the weapons importance in relation to value, and the skill required using your weapon of choice.

Van always told us before we began ...

"" Patience is a virtue of persistence! ""

Then he explained to master these toys reflect upon you writings of calligraphy.

Each movement is delicate and graceful in sight, but precise and deadly in format.

After our time was spent with this we always finished with a game of hide and seek.

We were encouraged to use our toys if we wished, because self-control was our domain.

After all of us had our turns being the seeker it was now time for rest.

Because morning was creeping up to us before we even realized it was already the next day.

Chapter ten

A Change in Routine

Again the time passed away, and now these children were young adults.

Meanwhile all these years in passing the outside world was becoming more and more harsh.

The noted politicians had become fat from their own greed overflowing their pockets, and our government is now so corrupt that it cracked!

Losing complete power to what now was the modern time drug lords.

The law was no more. Being in law-enforcement only meant that you and your family would have a better chance of survival in this new World.

As for the military there were only a few special groups. However they too were small in numbers and choose to hide among the shadows.

The only profitable means of living a good life was being that of a scientist, because they were held in the highest demand to produce many experimental projects.

But instead of using animals in their testing's they now began to conduct horrible procedures with us!

We the human race was now the official lab rats. This all was being performed unwillingly of course.

People and their whole families were disappearing all the time! As if it was a natural everyday occurrence.

And no one would even bat an eyelash. They merely only spoke under their own breath:

"Well we will get to see tomorrow once more at least?"

The appearance of the people now was starting to change as well. They now began to look something like that of a metamorphosis.

This was a direct result from the medical testing in the labs from the scientist's.

Back on the island things were still the same, and Sam and Silver knew nothing about the outside World of today.

Perhaps only slight distant memories of early childhood at best.

Their programming had just about been completed, and the time was drawing nearer for Van to unleash the harsh truth of the outside World to them.

As well as their purpose to aid in the re-discovery of mankind and that of pure human nature.

On the first eve of the last month of the year now being 2022 was the night for Sam and Silver to learn the truth.

After the lighting of the flickering flame these young adults began to prepare for fun time.

However; Van had other more important things in store for the two of them.

Van said: *"Sam ... Silver ... The time has come for you to truly understand as well as to realize your full purpose in life.*

Starting from this night you will have exactly one year to prepare for your journey that now lay ahead of you that was predetermined for you both to endure.

It will be the coming of your ages on your twenty-first birthday celebrations. ""

As Van spoke to them about the cruel World beyond the safety of their island home Sam and Silvers eyes began to widen quickly!

For this was a whole lot to absorb in only one night. Could this be true?

My sister and I were to be the chosen ones to save the World.

A World that we barely even knew in the least especially with all that had transpired.

Chapter eleven

Trails by Water

The very next morning breakfast was awaiting Sam and Silver, but Van was nowhere to be found.

Curiously they both set out to search the usual places on the island, but still no sign of Van.

So then they started their daily routine as normal, and assumed their push-up position on the top of the ridge by the volcano …

Next the ground began to quake and then the brightest light they ever seen aroused from the center of the amber glow of the molten lava below!

Just then a burst of hot heavy mist came to the top of the ridge.

Emerging from a mist was their mentor Van. Sam and Silver couldn't believe their own eyes!

A look of puzzlement to dismay they looked at one another first then peer at Van.

My children last night I laid a heavy blow to you about the World we live in, and today I must show you the rest including me.

Grasp my hands and come with me to see your real place of birth.

So without hesitation Sam and Silver took Vans hands. The next thing they knew they were in a small village by the sea.

Sam... Silver ... I know you can hardly believe what is happening, but I assure you it is real.

This is far too great a power for mere ordinary humans to accept, but you two are different aren't you?

Now is the time for which you always must have considered and I think now you can realize this fact.

We are in a place known as Zenzar bar. It is located at the center sphere of the World we live in.

This however is a magical place. A very unique and special place it is.

You see many years ago I arrived here un-knowing to its people.

This village and everyone who lives here is for the most part unrealized by the rest of the outside World around us.

Tonight at the torch lighting ceremony I will reveal all to you as to my true idenity.

As for now we must go to the great well of the village.

As they followed Van to the passage of the great water fall, and this well he spoke of… the villagers along the path stopped and knelt down in his presents.

It was an odd feeling not to mention that these were also the first people they ever saw besides that of themselves.

Then Van told the children … "" *all that we do each and every day is a reflection of Zen. Zen is totality and totality is all.* ""

The entire Universe that lay before you is comprised of what is called Ying and Yang.

Ying & Yang are the spheres of our great Universe as we know it today?

Representing all that is good is depicted as the white side, and all that is evil depicted by the dark side.

In order to co - exist and complement one another each has a speck of the other within their structure of sight.

This particular speck of color is the dot representing the eye of each opposing force.

This in whole is what makes up the entire sphere of what is Ying and Yang.

This reasoning is due to a belief that not all good is without some evil, and likewise not all evil is without some good nature about.

This symbol is supposed to represent two polar energies in which by their fluctuation to interactive activities from another cause our Universe to revolve.

This revolve statement literally means to exist within the realms of reality as we know it so far anyway. Until the time comes for us all to be enlightened unto what lies ahead of us.

Now the line which separates these two opposing forces is the grounds to merge one into another at will, and then by separating the halves self-showing this constant interaction to each other's force of opposition.

Whether this symbol be simple, or that of a cosmic phenomenon it characterizes many actions to re – actions. Be it in energy or human in reflection of itself.

Here is a simple list of Ying and Yang for you to try and grasp their meaning just a little bit better.

Ying & Yang

Night ~ Day
Winter ~ summer
Weak ~ Strong
Left ~ Right

So to realize the term of Ying and Yang it is all about opposites coming together.

Attracting first then splitting separating apart to create a harmonious state of being. This is Ying and Yang.

Welcome my children to the Great Well of power!

Its mystical properties run deep with intrigue as well as integrity. Come and meditate with me by the side of this Great Well.

As they next kneeled down before this spirited well it started to glow and swirl about!

You need to focus now even harder than you have ever done before to unlock great powers from within yourselves.

During your meditation, because with the help of this special well you can actually move from place to place.

Eventually you both will be able to go anywhere that you can imagine in the whole Universe threw your practice of meditation.

Remember my students the key to all victories in your life both in battle and oneself begin and end with patience.

This is called the Power of Will. It is quite powerful. Even more so than I.

This new skill you will learn will require much to master. You will learn as you go from this point on.

However; you will accomplish this, and also you must keep up with all of your daily current routines too.

So practice now like you have never have practiced before, and always know that no matter what I will always be proud of you both.

Chapter twelve
The Unveiling

The night came particularly quick with anticipation. Sam and Silver had so many questions now that their minds were close to imploding!

The entire last week had been a total culture shock for them both.

The man they called Van… the travel of meditation… the village… the well of course, and now the awaiting of the final shred of irony!

The torches of light were lit, and dinner was now being served. There was music being played to celebrate our arrival.

The overall mood was very pleasing. Yet still the wonder was overpowering our curiosity.

Van had then appeared once more what seemed to be out of nowhere!

My daughter Sam and my son Silver welcome to Zenzar Bar. This was your original place of birth.

To all the good people of Zenzar Bar my peace and safety of comfort shall always be with you.

If you remember me I walked through this village the day the visitors came from the sky.

Although I must say this wasn't my first time among you either? You see I have many abilities for which I will now disclose to you all at this time.

For one I 'am actually 1,200 years old! Sam glanced over at Silver ...

Second I may take the shape of any form that I wish. Shape shifting into anyone or anything in this World.

Eyes next grew wide as you could hear the heart's pumping from excitement.

Especially for Sam and Silver who were in a state of dismay to say in the least.

Before I continue let me show you may true form. Van took of his hat, and his eyes were glowing fiery red.

A burst of dark smoke pungent in smell filled the air we breathed, and a terrible sound echoed through the village!

The minds of all who were here gasped in fear even though they knew Van was their protector.

There he stood. Van was a Dragon God! A legend of myth; a fairytale of real life standing before us all!

Don't be frightened of me my children. I' am a friend to you all. The villagers began to chant loudly as they bowed down unto his presents.

Sam and I felt like we were made of stone and frozen in time. Then Van continued to speak.

Having great compassion for Mankind I feel pity for its downfall due to the unbalanced force of evil.

The spoken seven deadly sins of: Greed; Gluttony; Envy; Sloth; Wrath; Pride; and Lust.

These all need to be re-aligned, and the balance of the Universe also needs to be restored!

Sam and Silver you have been chosen by me for this task many years ago.

Although you were brought up as sister and brother you in fact are not.

You came from two different mothers, but you are both also my only and sole children.

You see I may only lie but a single egg in my life time span of 1,500 years, but I may change into human form and try to imp regent as many women as I can.

The only problem is that not all women are capable of carrying my seed. They may only do this one time.

It takes an extremely special woman to bear my children, and out of 1,200 years you two are my ones and only.

So now on your twenty-first birthday's you will come into all your true powers.

You will have the best of both Worlds in being human, but having Dragons blood in your chemistry too.

You will never age after your twenty-first birthdays ever again.

However you do need to keep up with all your training in both mind and body to lead your spirit's to great wisdom in the aid of Mankind.

The downfall to this all is that as like me you too will only live for 1,500 years. To continue our legacy you must also at some time bear children too.

We will talk soon about all the other powers that will befall you once you have reached the day of empowerment.

Chapter thirteen
Before The Turning

The night seemed as if it were a never ending dream. So much has happened all at once that it became overwhelming.

But the next day it was right back into the normal flow of our routines.

We were taken to the Great Well by Van every night. In order for us to work our technique in time traveling by the art of meditation.

To accomplish this feat we only had but to focus either on a particular name or place, and when we opened our eyes we were there in or at the place we thought of.

The first time we went back to our own island, and it didn't take long before this came easy to us.

Then we went back and forth between the island and our new home the village of Zenzar Bar.

Our bodies became stronger and more agile with each passing day. Our minds became more focused and visual.

With the two of these aspects combined together our spirits soared as if we were riding the wind.

This was the Dragon spirit within us preparing to come into age. Then one evening very close to our twenty first birthdays Van took us to a place he called New Orleans.

He told us that this was a spawning ground for the evil that spread over the lands.

Not knowing what to really expect we expected the worst.

By doing this we would be-able to move forward quicker once we evaluated the situation for our self's.

But we were not here to begin our quest, but rather to see what lies before us to correct the balance.

Upon our return back to the island we were told we need to always remember that we were a team.

Also that to fight against this evil would be hurtful at first, because of what we must do to prevail.

We would have to battle to the very end of time until this evil was vanquished.

Along the way we would make some allies and new friendships which would prove useful in this time ahead of us.

No matter what may happen or what we might see to always be aware of the signs to guide us.

Chapter fourteen

The Coming of Age

The time for us had finally arrived! Everything that we worked so hard for, and had become from our countless dedication now we were ready to go forth and accept our destiny.

We then started the day on our beloved Island of Ryu Kyu once more with our usual routine that we were accustomed to.

While at the Working Tree Sam and I couldn't help but to ponder. Would we ever see this place we called home ever again?

To what degree would we have to go to do what had been placed before us to accomplish?

Lastly how this mission would affect each of us for the rest of our lives?

As evening approached us we traveled back to Zenzar Bar.

Upon our appearance we were met with a spectacular festival to celebrate our coming of age.

There was music, entertainment, great food, and what we had realized to be good friends.

It seemed all too good to be true. What a way to celebrate our birthdays.

All the while knowing that at some point during this fantastic ceremony of sorts that we would both be begging our journey to save the World.

All of a sudden ... Everything stopped! There was nothing except dead silence.

Van now at the head of the great fire stood up. He then announced that it was now time, and then he changed his shape back to his original Dragon form.

He looked like a mythic God! Next he called us forward to stand before him.

As we approached gingerly... we began to feel a dramatic change! Our bodies transformed into tigers.

My children said Van. In the beginning your animal form shall be that of the tiger.

As you both mature from wisdom with new knowledge over time underneath your feet you will then be transforming into that of young Dragons.

This is The Martial Way! Let experience by thy guide.

To blend into your surroundings you may however adapt and change into any form of a human or lessor animal forms to secure your identity.

Next we were given gifts that were specially handcrafted from the villagers. They were traditional weapons of the orient culture.

These were our extension of arm besides that of our self-defense techniques we were taught.

Then we knelt at the Great Well. As we started to accept our fate the pool of water began to stir.

Then it had a bubbling glow of an eerie sight! As two spirits came forth!

It was the spirit of our Universe Ying and Yang. As they spiraled above us and spoke of the past; present; and our future we next stared into the eyes of the abyss.

Then Sam and I were set forth and disappeared from sight of our father.

Farewell my children. My peace comes from your effort of character!

~ New York & Los Angeles ~

The End?

The Elders Book II
The Elders Book II

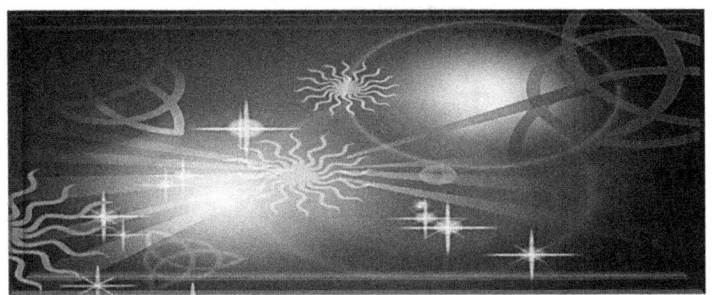

By:

Michael P. Faraday

Chapters

1. Origins

2. The Five Rings

3. Virtues of color

4. Pure form

5. Temple of the Dragons

6. Power of knowledge

7. Testing the waters

8. into the mouth of madness

9. Separating from statures

10. Preparations

11. Foresight

12. The perfection of beauty

13. A new age

Quote:

"I will not conform to the man; but the man shall conform to me! "

By:

Kyoshi Michael P. Faraday

Preface

Before this World was even ever existed there was an ominous sea of dark space for which the only light that shown were of five bright glowing clusters.

These clusters of light were known to one another as the Five Rings. Through their vision the Universe as we think we know it came to be.

One in particular speck of dust they deemed Earth! As time evolved so did this World.

The rise and fall of many have passed, and the history in stories was vast in nature.

However; it was little to be known that the one single truth was that we were in fact created by these Gods.

Purely for their enjoyment only, and when the certain day came that this dream was done …

Then so shall we! This is where the idealism of fait comes into play. For the soul of man is by far the most valuable creation of all.

For when the Mind joins the body the power that it creates is our soul!

EARTH

Elements

Are

Relative

To

Hope!

Chapter one

Origins

Through the span of time we have seen documentation from the rise and fall of many empires.

Their ruthless leaders of dictatorship and slavery accompanied by their harsh laws were brutal!

These so called self-proclaimed figures couldn't even endure the pain that they unleashed.

The lands were tarnished with the blood stained soil from wars without purpose except for that of self-gain.

There was no real honor to glory or empowerment of balance. There were merely the loud cries as the shadows of Death marched fourth.

Taking whatever may have held interest or may have amused them at the time leaving everything else in total dismay to destruction.

However a small "Silver" of light bore through these dark shadows. The cries where heard from an ever so few brave souls.

These became to be known our heroes to legends from myths of the old wise tales told by our Elders.

But let it be known that every story no matter how it's lined out has distinct clues to that of partial truth for all of us to follow!

Chapter two

The Five Rings

The balance to all harmony is centered from the core of the Universe. This is represented by the Talisman of the Ying and Yang.

In ancient beliefs of oriental culture this Talisman has been forged into many different colors as well as in depiction of its own self.

The inner secrets to it is said to elaborate that of five dragons. These dragons are as told:

"White ~ Black ~ Green ~ Silver and Red. "

The key to this whole so called talisman is that whoever may hold the inner gift granted to them by death and take into their possession shall never know what side will ever overcome them more?

The light side representing all that is good, or the dark side which is the circumference to pure evil!

Then again depending on the person it reflects may suffer an evenly split right down the sphere of the middle between the two.

Chapter three

Virtues of colors

The White Dragon is called; Heaven, and is made up of all that is good. In his thoughts his actions are pure as well as they are just.

The Black Dragon is called; Van, and has a shadowy past. His heart is good, but his means are never clear as to his intensions.

The Green Dragon is called; Envy and he is never happy unless his power is equal to his brothers. He is measured from his peers by the ponds he plays in life.

The Silver Dragon is the only one whose power is split equal to his existence.

Although he reflects both the light and the dark he is also ultimately the most powerful dragon of all hands down! He is known plainly as just Silver.

Now last but not least the Red Dragon is called Hell; and he enjoys his temper far more than his love in any and all lines drawn. It is he who acts first out of his hatred.

V

The Five Dragons

The Silver Dragon

SILVER

HEAVEN

The White Dragon

ENVY

The Green Dragon

HELL

The Red Dragon

VAN

The Black Dragon

Chapter four

Pure form

Before the age of man who was created for the sole purpose of amusement there were five supreme beings that were in fact immortal.

They were seen as bright Hugh masses of glowing pure energy. This was the light of the inner darkness.

These masses of light lingered among the center point of what we today call our Universe.

It was these beings who created us all and everything we know of today. This idealism is known as Zen.

Zen defined in philosophy means that all is totality and totality is all!

These five Gods referred to one another as Silver, Heaven, Envy, Hell and Van.

They considered themselves to be fierce dragons. Each of these dragons was an all wise fierce entity who had no bounds to laws of nature or of physics.

When speaking the dragon gods used the powers of telepathy, because to hear the sound of their true voice was said to unleash vast destruction.

When not gathered all together they enjoyed creating other lesser forms of life to occupy their time.

It is this act for which history became recorded.

For when these five immortals created man the turning point to oblivion was inevitable!

You see all games must come to an end, but it is how they end that is the biggest question for us all?

For it has been many centuries that have past now and during the millennium the Dragons are becoming bored once more.

A change is on the horizon. One eve that hasn't even been foreseen not even by the elders themselves.

When this does cometh to be; not even these great Gods will be able to prevent the occurrence!

Chapter five

Temples of the Dragons

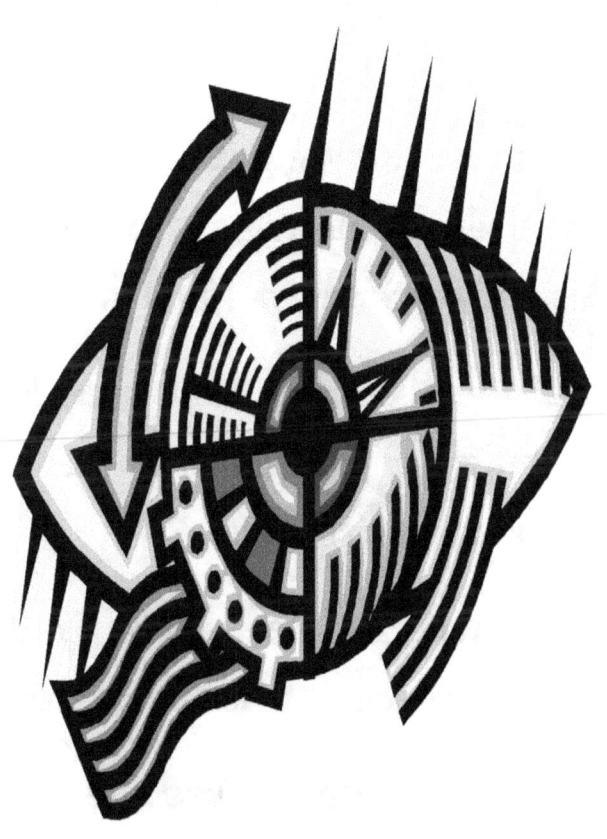

For reasons only known to the Dragons Earth was their favorite creation of life.

Spanning around the World they each had built a special place for which they gathered to plot the ponds of their game called life.

Never truly knowing the purpose of these ancient ruins we as humans refer to these places as mysterious in origin.

Each of these temples had a medallion of its creator embedded into the center most part of its structure.

Only one who has been chosen can see the true existence of these medallions.

Because to that of the naked eye they are invisible, But if you were indeed special this is what you might briefly see?

The Five Temples of the Dragons were: Easter Island, The Mayan Ruins, Stone Hedge, the Egyptian Pyramids, and the Great Wall of China.

It is here where their essence can be found for all of us to see in plain sight.

However that is by far the best part of all, because there is no trace of them whatsoever to see!

All that remains are these relics of old ancient ruins just waiting for the right individual to unlock their real secrets of intension.

How they are found and exactly what their secrets hold is yet to become.

For nothing is easily accomplished in life without hard work.

Once this discovery is made a new beginning will commence for he who holds all the medallions will become the one and only supreme ruler of all in this World and of others too.

The lost Temples of the Dragons:

The Silver Dragon

~ Temple of Light ~

Silver

The White Dragon

~ Temple of Souls ~

Heaven

The Green Dragon

~ Temple of Greed ~

Envy

The Red Dragon

~ Temple of Shadows ~

Hell

The Black Dragon

~ Temple of Thought ~

Van

Chapter six

Power of knowledge

In the eternal battle for supreme power it was then discovered by Van the Black Dragon that he himself could produce off spring.

With his new creation in that of women if he himself took their form of being.

Once he realized all the effects of this discovery he did everything that he could to keep this his secret from his brothers.

For now the upper hand lay towards him. However like in any other new creation he had to wait, and discover the pros, and the cons to the planting of his seed with that of a mortal being. Could it be possible for a mortal woman to carry and to birth a child of a God?

Being that of Immortal was one thing but being mortal another. The cause and effect of one species integrating with the opposite had yet to be determined!

Chapter seven

Testing the Waters

Traveling the lands as a Nomad Van tried to cloak him-self so as not to attract attention from that of his brothers in regards to his new plan.

What better a way than to become nobody? Then to become a person who can come and go as they wished, and remain undetected by everyone in plain sight.

He found a new love in walking beside the mortals in what his brother Envy created as The Orient.

Van found this place to be Enchanting and in the same time the mysterious ora's which encompassed its people.

For the most part they were a simple class of people who on the other hand had quite a sophisticated means of self-defense.

They called this Martial Science which was the harnessing of {KI} which was their inner strength and then learning how to project it in an outward fashion creating a weapon out of their own bodies.

This was paired with the science of understanding the intricate points of vitality within a human body structure evolved into an equation of physics.

This system of self-defense enabled us to distinctly demobilize their aggressor until their demise!

Even though Van was a Dragon God he found a tremendous satisfaction in learning this Martial Science from the people he had helped create with his brothers.

Van thought to himself ... Imagine the day has finally come for changes when the creator learns from that of his creations!

He found it to not only be relaxing, but fancied its finesse into warfare as well. Humbling was this feeling of new indulgence.

As he regularly took ritual in meditation this all became clear one evening near a small village secluded by an enchanting waterfall he then envisioned this new found love as the ultimate revenge against his fellow brothers.

By enhancing the knowledge of his very own existence and the rituals he had now learned from their creations what if he could now be able to create his own offspring someday with that of a mortal woman?

He next thought once more to himself …
… By creating this hybrid of myself paired with this new found knowledge, and then adding some power of focus a worthy opponent for which would defy all known nature would daze and

confuse any who may stand before them!

Alas ... As long as I can shadow the existence of this new force the ways of this World can at last be free?

My brothers and I have played the game for too long! It's time for a new beginning with this my final gift of creation to this World.

I shall call this the {Do}. This is intended to mean the way. Then at a young age once they have been nurtured by the mortal mother I will then return, and begin my teaching to them this Martial Science.

This will in return enhance the fusion of their bodies to their spirits making their minds equal to that of my own.

So then they may see and learn the true potential of their inner powers which dwell within them, for which are not that of mortal man.

It is at this crucial point that this new breed shall be set free to hopefully bring balance back into this Universe.

~ {Bodi} Body ~

~ {Makeaki} Spirit ~

~ {Omi} Mind ~

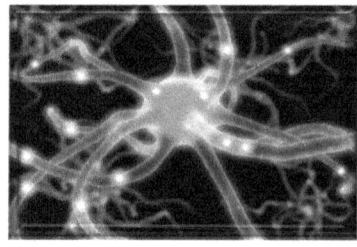

Chapter eight

Into the mouth of madness

Several years now had pasted by and The Five Rings had not gathered at their temples leaving them fall to ruin.

From the art of shape shifting into whatever forms they wished became so much fun to do that none of them knew where the others were.

Nevertheless who or what they were either!

This became a total chaos, and drove these all mighty Gods out of their own supremacy so to speak.

Sheltered into existence they each were able to build secret empires that went un-noticed.

The major plan was to create a loyal following to lead into this epic final war to become the only one who would rein superior without challenge, and find the way to extinguish the essence of the remaining brothers.

Chapter nine

Separating from statures

At a period of time when the creation of man was at its most vulnerable and impressionable state of mind these Gods infected human kind with subliminal suggestion of thought.

The White Dragon and the Red Dragon build the ideal of the kingdoms of Heaven and Hell!

This very conception was relevant to morality of good vs. evil, and leads those who were followers into a line of compliance.

The other three remaining Gods thought of this as a washing of the mind, and called it belief of religion.

So with this implanting was set forth the everlasting movement of the perils of the Religious War also referred to as the Holy Wars!

Having no fond love of these new found invoked powers over man Van set forth to dwell the lands in self-exile without a face of distinction.

By doing this he had lots of time to not only think, but also to learn from the mistakes of himself and those of his brothers from their past revelations.

Before Van even realized how long he had actually been living among men in secret... hundreds of years had now pasted by.

The other four Gods had actually all but forgotten about him due to their own self indulgencies.

This made it all the more easier for Van to pursue the execution of his master plan which was to restore the balance back into this World that he and his brothers had created.

The Black Dragon had found his new love of inspiring nature in what again was referred to as The Orient.

He witnessed as well as observed for the longest of time the hardships of man, and how their skills expanded from that of Martial Science.

Martial Science is the essence of balance within one's body, and then projected into harmony.

This develops with patience as the spirit strengthens the body and the mind next fuses together and together act as one.

Simple put this translates into a set of specific equations into that of learning the mechanics of the human body, or as I call them physics.

In the theories of this Martial Science it is intended for the pupil to one day become the master and the master to become a legend.

Meanwhile the Green Dragon Envy disappeared across the seas and began his new reign in The Emerald Isles.

His army was to be built on the souls of greed and misfortune so to create a lavish decent of morality of dark beliefs he then build a kingdom of castles overlooking the horizons.

It is from his eye that the mystical myths of Leprechauns, Banshees, trolls, Sprites, and Sirens became a reality.

What better a way to impose rule from that of fears then by tales of horrible truths from eyewitness accounts.

Beneath the land his World was born as he next continued to develop temporary portholes to go back and forth between for his interests of travel.

The Trolls build his empire in the caverns and guarded his portholes of travel from all who discovered their existence.

The Banshees were used to lore the lost souls of lust that wandered about the countryside into slavery.

The Sprites were used to steal children and force them into early slavery as well.

Then the Sirens guarded the shores of the Isle from all that may pose a threat to the kingdom of the Green Dragon.

Lastly the Leprechauns were used to lore their victims from that of trickery.

Little by little man was subdued by these dark forces and the legends they immersed brought fear across the lands!

For now a new age of darkness had rose with that of dark forces to be called upon to do their bidding.

So with all of this Envy was indeed pleased and had no need to trespass the safety of the borders he created, or at least for the time being.

The only Dragon left was the Silver Dragon. Because of his even split of power the others thought of him as no threat, but as like that of insanity.

So Silver was always referred to as the philosophical blabbering fool that spoke in twisted logic.

However it was the Silver Dragon who built the great Mayan Ruins. Although the others once again laughed in his face they were unable to fully understand why he chose to build this enormous walkway to the stars.

To Silver this was a soothing place for meditation. Also let it be known that this was the highest point in the entire World at one point in time, and everyone and everything was always within his view of sight.

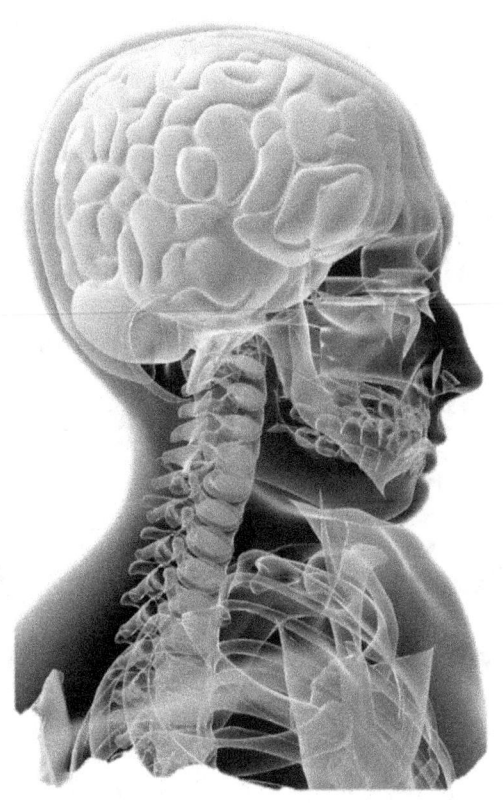

Chapter ten

Preparations

Before the Black Dragon began to set his master plan into action he decided to erect what became the Great Wall of China.

The purpose of this wall was to protect that of the Orient for which he came to love so much, and to slowdown the plague of the rising evils to the western World to come.

For between this and The United States there was nothing, but fuel to stem the fires.

The model of this would be like that of a hurricane that was gathering moisture for massive destruction.

You see the true meaning of knowledge is power and the more you know to understanding is to how much more powerful you will become.

Next Van began his long journey into the search of balance in learning this Martial Science from those that were created by himself along with his brothers.

The Human race was evolving even more quickly than the Gods ever had imagined. The time for capturing capital expansion was for the taking if you know what I mean?

For the time being he didn't consider himself to be even a God, but rather he cloaked himself as monk and remained among men.

Never did he reveal his face and he became known as the monk without a shadow.

Why a monk of all choices do you ask? Very simple because who would ever conceive to expect a mere religious man sheltered within a temple to actually be a real God.

One who in fact was planning an epic revolt against his savage selfish brothers to save the World? No one would not even another God this is by far irony at its best!

So with his idea of simplicity he blended in. For another hundred years or so, and then during this time he spent all of it learning as well as perfecting what he could once again from the creation of man that were placed in the dimension we call Earth.

There is so much knowledge out there that has yet to be discovered, and yet even still more for which we ourselves just are not ready to comprehend.

Simple put this would just blow our minds!

Chapter eleven

Foresight

As dawn began to break the temple of The Tiger came alive with sounds of clatter. Although no one ever spoke to one another in words; they understood each other by ones facial expressions through the day.

While deep into meditation Vans eyes opened wide as soon as he heard these sounds, and then his senses could smell breakfasts being prepared.

You see Gods never sleep. They do not require all the necessities that we do.

So he used this time to plan and to think about how to come to terms with the future he had envisioned to one day unfold.

Looking down this great path from the Tiger Temple to the mountains on the eastern ridge it was a long winding path that led to the evergreen forest to the place where the sun burned off the early morning mist.

The day had now begun. At the temple it was now time to learn from the blood, sweat, and also the tears of tribulations of trails from yet another glorious day!

Although words were never permitted to be spoken here they were replaced with that of wood smacking against wood and bones smashing against bone!

To feel pain was to be alive and the more you felt alive the more weakness had left your body to make that of your spirit stronger.

In other words your mind and your body were fusing together making your spirit the temple for your soul.

You had learned to appreciate the more simple tasks of life finding the beauty of splendor from that of achievement of hard work!

The act of great achievement is defined as the effort of much hard work became the mechanism of Kung-Fu.

The sands of time slowly dropped grain by grain in the hourglass. The years had now passed by as if time it self-stood still.

Living in this type of solitude paired among these fine people truly humbled Van.

He had not only witnessed the true ora of the Human spirit for the goodness it kept, but he also felt the dark side of his past blooming with a new thought of love and compassion!

It was at this point he knew it was time to begin phase two of his master plan, and put his seed so to speak of secret into this World.

{This is a Chinese symbol for secret.}

Chapter twelve

The perfection of beauty

Now wandering all across creation the Black Dragon was in search of a perfect woman one who could perhaps bare his offspring?

If this was to be possible they would be nothing in essence that this World has ever seen.

Although these beings would appear to be normal they in actuality would be greatly different with amazing hidden powers of talent.

The big question would be how long would it take for them to achieve their full potentials in all growth areas, and exactly how many offspring could he produce being a God.

Van found out extremely quick that not all women were created equal, and to complete phase two it would take an exceptional special woman to do just this.

After much disappointment Van himself became weary and started to wonder about revising his thoughts.

The first couple of hosts were unable to carry to a full term and with this both mother and child were lost around the seventh month of conception.

It was unfortunate but this held true for the next and the next after that along with several more tries after.

With great disappointment once more Van sought absolute solitude.

The World was beginning to change, and even still becoming more advanced with more horror and bloodshed for personal gain!

So much time had passed again that not only had the Black Dragon been long forgotten, but the Silver and Green Dragons too.

It was the Red and White Dragons who reign supreme and took on permanent human forms.

Along with new names, but reaped the almighty benefits of still being known to be God's.

Their conceptions of tricks of the mind collected many souls to keep! It was in fact a known truth to them that it was these souls which became to be the most valuable of all.

These souls of the human race they had created along with their other brothers.

For the time being The Five Rings had all but been forgotten and written into scripture.

The two Gods were depicted into the White Dragon known as God, and the Red Dragon as being the Devil!

Good vs. Evil

Chapter thirteen

A new age

The legends of old have become myths because these incidents' of topic had happened so long ago.

Horrid tales of all the Folklores mystical creatures that stole children in the mists of the night became night time tale's for small children before bedtime.

All these stories of reality were cast off into nothing more than mere bedtime stories of make believe.

Unknowingly there was such a time in history for which all these stories were in fact all too real!

Now all the new horrors of man were depicted against him-self for reasons unknown by him, but were created by religions from the Red and the White Dragons.

For their own personal amusement had commenced with the fears and doubts from their installations of faiths.

It started with Alcohol in what became known as the Era of Prohibition, and then graduated into the World Wars.

As the decades past the violence of man spread like a cancer. It spider webbed into separate entities.

The tactics of man were now even more evolved, and the death tolls rose higher and more brutal then the ones before.

During these periods Van found that to conceal his true idenity was no longer an easy task.

The time for vengeance grew nearer, but to find refuge was harder. Then during his nightly meditations Van had two startling new visions which broke his concentration!

In the first vision Van saw a jungle that led to an enchanted waterfall. As his spirit drifted pass this obstacle he then saw off in the distance a glowing well of unspeakable powers.

These powers were unconceivable even to Van and gave a strong feeling of uneasiness to his existence!

Standing next to the well were two women who carried large vases filled with sorrow for which they dumped into this sacred well.

As Van looked on he had glanced upon the beauty of the woman's eyes which drew him ever so more closely.

Then he heard them speak each other's names. One was called Alexandria and the other was named Anita.

These particular women were unlike any of the other women Van had ever met. Alexandria and Anita were very special if you know what I mean?

Next the word Zenzar bar kept flashing in Vans mind. Trying to explore deeper into his meditation a great storm began to brew.

The clouds darkened. The wind had picked up and blew like a freight train. Between the cracks of heavy lighting he could see the twisting funnel of death dropping skeleton faces of men of war!

As the shroud of darkness fell over the land a very bright light burst from the epicenter, and here stood the clearest vision Van had ever seen.

The experience was so overwhelming that his breath fell short! It was of no consequence that Van was a God.

Instantly Van quickly realized this was going to be the ultimate new power of the entire Universe!

As this light overtook and cast out the darkness of evil there stood a family of three warriors.

This family of true virtue stood on a small sandy beach hidden from the sight of the rest of the World.

Van opened his eyes which suffered an act of R.E.M. associated with continued shortness of breath from this vision, and then Van spoke three final names ...

QuickSilver, Sam, and Mason Storm!

The End?

"" *Overlooking a city of Angeles the red glow of the cries from the hollows below screamed out into the night!*

As the Moons light shined bright across his blade high in the hills of what used to bear the sign Hollywood... Silver set forth to begin his first journey alone? *""*

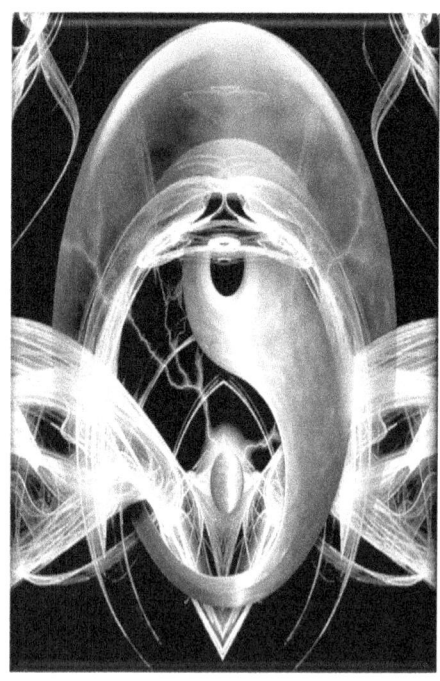

The legend will continue...

Acknowledgements

All the characters based in The Legend of QuickSilver series are fictional and sole property of QuickSilver The Silver Dragon Inc., and Michael P. Faraday.

Cast of Characters

Van:

Is a wandering nomad that is actually a God? Van has great disappointment in his brothers the other Gods, but unlike him they have no compassion for that of mankind.

I choose this character in recognition of my teacher from his spiritual guidance that he bestows on me. I address him as Shidoshi, but he is an actual legend in the Martial arts today and he is Ron "The Black Dragon" Van Clief.

Sam:

This character is based on my wife Tammy who is constantly on my mind along with my son Mason.

Later on in this series there will be a character to represent my son as well.

Being actually brought up into a life of Martial Arts by my father-in-law Mr. Ray Barnes my wife has been involved in the Oriental Culture in some shape or form since the 1970's.

This particular character Sam is a young woman who unknowingly is preparing to follow the code of ethics in The Martial Way to aid in the compassion of Mankind.

Sam is also a nickname that I call her quite frequently.

Silver:

This character is based on ideals from vast trials and tribulations into real life events paired with a science fiction twist to make entertaining from my life.

I have walked the path of Living the Martial Way since the age of twelve, & currently hold the rank of Kyoshi which is a 7th degree black belt.

I have traveled the World with my training, competitions, & teachings in Martial Science.

My nickname is Q.S. / QuickSilver the Silver Dragon, & you may find out more information about me @ the following web address:

www.quicksilverthesilverdragoninc.com

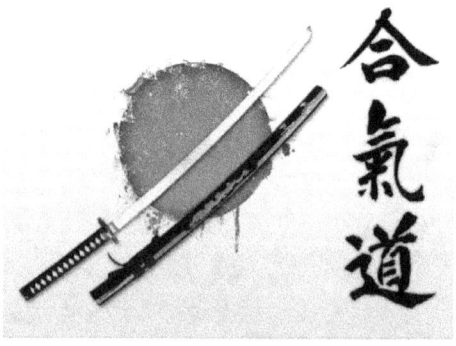

I on this 25th day of February 2015 fully dedicate this book to my beloved son Mason D. Faraday.

It is always a pleasure in listening to the many stories that my son makes up and tells me, and with that I hope he really enjoys mine.

All my best:

~ *Quicksilver* ~

Michael P. Faraday

$ 14.95